Published by Sweet Cherry Publishing Limited
Unit 36, Vulcan House,
Vulcan Road,
Leicester, LE5 3EF
United Kingdom

First published in the UK in 2019
2019 edition

2 4 6 8 10 9 7 5 3 1

ISBN: 978-1-78226-413-2

© Sweet Cherry Publishing

Sherlock Holmes: The Speckled Band

Based on the original story from Sir Arthur Conan Doyle,
adapted by Stephanie Baudet.
Cover Design by Arianna Bellucci and Rhiannon Izard
Illustrations by Arianna Bellucci

www.sweetcherrypublishing.com

Printed in India
I.IPP001

SHERLOCK HOLMES

THE SPECKLED BAND

SIR ARTHUR CONAN DOYLE

Sweet
Cherry
PUBLISHING

For the past eight years it has been my habit to record the cases I have worked on with my friend, Sherlock Holmes. These cases have been sometimes tragic,

occasionally comic, and *never* ordinary. Since Holmes worked for the love of his craft rather than money, he refused to take on any case that was anything less than unusual. His approach to his work was very simple: the stranger the case, the greater his pleasure.

Glancing over my notes, I can find no case stranger than that concerning the speckled band, which until now I have been unable to write about.

6

Back then a pledge of secrecy to a young lady prevented me from adding the case to the archive. Now her sad passing frees me from that promise so that I might finally tell the truth about the death of Doctor Grimesby Roylott, and quieten much wild rumour and speculation.

It was in early April of the year 1883 and still early in our friendship when I was awoken by Mr Sherlock Holmes standing fully dressed by the side of my bed. He was normally a late riser and I blinked at the clock on the mantelpiece, which read seven-fifteen, with surprise and a little annoyance. I was usually quite regular in my habits and this was earlier than my usual time of rising.

'Apologies for disturbing you, Watson,' he said with a rueful smile. 'We have all been woken early; first Mrs Hudson, then me.'

'What is it, Holmes? A fire?'

'No, a client. A very frightened young lady has arrived and insists on seeing me. She is in the living-room. If she is up and about at such an early hour it must be something urgent. I know how you like to follow cases from the beginning, so I thought I would give you the choice of staying in bed or coming in to hear her story.'

'My dear fellow, I wouldn't miss it for anything,' I said, now wide awake and excited at the idea of a new mystery to solve. I had no greater pleasure than helping Holmes in his investigations as he searched for clues and logically found answers.

In a few moments I was dressed and we went downstairs to the living room.

The lady was dressed in black and wore a heavy veil over her face, making it difficult to see her clearly. She rose as we entered.

'Good morning, madam,' said Holmes cheerily. 'My name is

Sherlock Holmes and this is my friend and colleague, Doctor Watson. You may speak freely in front of him.'

He looked at the fire and for once acknowledged our landlady. 'Ha! I see that Mrs Hudson has had the good sense to light the fire. Pray come and sit beside it – you're shivering.

 These April mornings are still chilly. I will order you a cup of hot coffee.'

He rang for Mrs Hudson and she came and took our order for coffee as our client took her seat. Then, lifting her veil, the lady said, 'It is not the cold that makes me shiver, but the terror I face.'

This caught my attention and I studied her more closely. Her face was pale and her eyes restless with a frightened, haunted look to them. Although she must have been barely thirty, her hair was

12

already turning grey. She looked exhausted.

Holmes of course would have noted all these facts too, and probably made more of them than I did. I observed with a doctor's eye, he with that of a detective.

'You must not fear,' he said, soothingly. 'We shall soon put things right. You have come in by train this morning I see.'

She nodded, surprised.

Holmes continued, either not noticing her reaction or choosing to ignore it. 'You have your return ticket tucked into your left glove. You must have started early and had a long journey along heavy roads to the station in a dog-cart.'

The lady stared first at Holmes and then at her gloved hand, where I could now see the edge of the ticket poking out. I noted a hint of concern in her expression too, which was not surprising among people unfamiliar with Holmes' methods of deduction.

He smiled. 'There is no mystery, my dear. The left arm of your jacket is splattered with fresh mud.

Dog-cart

A simple wooden cart drawn by one horse and used on country estates. Some have a bench for the driver and one passenger, others have back-to-back seats. They have a tendency to throw mud onto the left side. Originally the rear seat folded down to make room for dogs, hence the name.

Only a dog-cart throws up mud like that, and then only when you sit on the left-hand side of the driver.'

'You are right, Mr Holmes.' Her features relaxed a little. 'I started out at six o'clock this morning from my home in Surrey.'

Suddenly a wave of concern overcame her and her face seemed to crumple. 'Oh sir, I shall go mad if this continues. I was recommended to you by a friend whom you helped. Her name is Mrs Farintosh, and she gave me your address,' the lady added in response to a quizzical look from Holmes. 'I beg you to help me too!'

Holmes took a casebook down from a bookshelf and idly leafed through it for a moment. 'Farintosh,' he mused. 'Ah, yes,  the opal tiara. Before your time, Watson,' he said over his shoulder.

Our client's puzzled expression gave way to mild irritation at

Holmes' apparent distraction. 'I cannot pay you immediately,' she went on, 'but I shall be married in a few weeks and will have my own income.'

'My job is my own reward,' said Holmes. 'But you may pay any expenses when you are able. Now please give us as much detail as you can about your situation. It is vital that we understand the matter before us. What do you fear?'

Our client breathed deeply as she attempted to calm herself before

18

beginning her story. 'It is difficult
to say what I fear as my suspicions
are vague. Some would say I am
just a nervous woman, but you,
sir, I know you can look deeper
and see the wickedness in people's
hearts. You can advise me how to
deal with these dangers.'

'I am listening, madam.'

I drew my chair nearer so as not
to miss a word.

'My name is Helen Stoner and
I live with my step-father,
Doctor Grimesby Roylott. He
is the last member of a once-

rich family that has owned a house called Stoke Moran for several hundred years. The family fortunes have long gone and all that is left is a crumbling house, a few acres of ground and a mortgage to pay. Generations of the family squandered their money and my step-father realised that he would need to establish himself in some profession.

'He earned a medical degree and went to India where he established a large and successful doctor's practice.

He married my
mother when my
twin sister, Julia,
and I were two
years old. For
a time he had
great success in Calcutta, but
that all ended when he killed his
butler in a fit of rage following
some robberies in our house. He
went to prison for a long time
and returned to England a very
sad and bitter man.'

Holmes nodded from time to
time and his face remained neutral.

I pondered, as I often did, how
he could show so little emotion
or reaction. I knew so little of
him in those early days of our
acquaintance.

'My mother had a good income,'
Miss Stoner continued, 'which
she gave to my step-father on the
condition that when Julia and I
married, a third of it should be
paid to each of us, leaving one
third for himself. Soon afterwards
my mother was killed in a train

accident and Doctor Roylott
decided to give up his attempts

22

at setting up a practice
in London. He took us to
live with him at Stoke Moran,
and we were happy for a time.
The money our mother left was
enough to cover any expenses
and Julia and I had each other.

It was around this time that
Doctor Roylott began to behave
oddly: he shut himself in the
house and saw no one. He would
fight with anyone who came near
the house and his temper was so
violent that everyone in the village
feared him. He is a very strong man.

Twice he has ended up in front
of the courts for fighting. Just
last week he hurled the local
blacksmith into the stream, and it
was only by paying the man all the
money I could find that
we were able to avoid yet
another scandal.

His only friends are
some vagabonds whom
he allows to camp in the
grounds. And then there
are the animals ...'

'Animals?' I asked, and she turned to face me.

'Yes, Doctor Watson. He brought back some wild animals from India. There is a cheetah and a baboon that are allowed to roam freely.'

At this point Mrs Hudson arrived with the coffee and I suspect she heard the last statement for she raised her eyebrows but said nothing.

Once she had left and the coffee had been poured, I asked,

'I assume your father's temper means you have difficulty retaining staff?'

'My sister and I did all the work. No one would stay once they witnessed his behaviour. We had no pleasure in our lives except for an occasional visit to our aunt in Harrow – my mother's sister. Then Julia died. She was only thirty years old, but her hair had already begun to turn white, just as mine has.'

Holmes had been sitting with his eyes closed but now they flicked open. 'Your sister is dead?'

27

'She died two years ago, and it is about her that I wish to speak to you. While visiting our aunt, Julia met a young major in the marines and they became engaged. Our step-father seemed to have no objection to this and all plans were made. But a fortnight before the wedding day, she died horribly. From that day I have had no company except that of my step-father.'

'Pray be precise with the details,' said Holmes.

'That is easy for me. Every

28

detail of that terrible night
is burned into my memory.'
Miss Stoner paused and fidgeted
with her dress for a moment
before returning to her narrative.

'I have drawn a plan of the
house to aid you, Mr Holmes.' She
took a piece of folded paper out
of her bag and laid it on a small
table in front of us before sipping
at her coffee.

'The house is so old and in such
poor condition that only one wing
is inhabited,' she said, pointing on
the plan. 'The three bedrooms are

on the ground floor with the sitting
rooms behind. Here is Doctor
Roylott's room, here is my sister's
next to it, and here is my own, the
third in the line.'

Holmes and I peered at the
plan. It was quite simple.

'They are accessed by a corridor but there is no link between the rooms themselves. The windows open out onto the lawn. Do you see?'

'Indeed,' said Holmes.

'On that fatal night Doctor Roylott went to his room early, although we know that he didn't go straight to bed because my sister could smell the strong Indian cigars he likes to smoke. She came into my room and we talked for a while about her wedding. It warmed

31

my heart to see how excited she was. At eleven o' clock she got up to leave but at the door she turned and said: "Helen, have you ever heard someone whistling in the middle of the night?" She said it with such seriousness that it took me rather by surprise and it was a few moments before I could answer.'

'I said I hadn't, and she told me that for the past few nights she had heard a low, clear whistle at about three o'clock in the morning. She couldn't tell where it came from and we thought maybe it was the vagabonds in the grounds. But then, surely, I would have heard it too, although I'm a heavier sleeper than she was. I don't expect it's very important. She went to her room then and I locked my door. I heard her do the same also.'

'Was it your habit to lock yourselves in at night?' Holmes asked.

I could see that this mystery had caught his imagination and he was listening to every word she said. To a stranger Holmes

may not always look as
though he is paying
attention, but I knew
that he was.

'Always,' she replied.

'Why?'

'Because of the
cheetah and the baboon.
We didn't feel safe unless
the doors were locked. I
still don't.'

Holmes nodded, and I
tried to imagine living somewhere
that had wild animals roaming
the grounds.

'I could not sleep that night,' went on Miss Stoner. 'I had a feeling that something awful was going to happen. As twins, Julia and I often knew what the other was thinking. Outside the sky raged and rain was beating and splashing against the windows. Suddenly, there was a terrified scream and I knew it was my sister's voice. I sprang out of bed, threw a shawl around my shoulders, and rushed into the corridor.'

She paused, her eyes reflecting

the terror she must have felt then.

'I heard the whistle and then, a short time later, a metallic clanging sound. My sister's door was opening slowly. In the dim light of the corridor lamp, I saw her emerge from her room, her face white with terror. Her hands were searching for something to grasp and I ran forwards and caught her before she fell, but I couldn't hold her up. She slipped to the floor and then writhed as if in great pain. I bent over to see if she was conscious and she stared at me and shrieked in a voice such as I have never heard before. I will *never* forget that voice.'

The woman in front of us shook in terror as she retold her dreadful story and I wondered what the past two years must have been like for her. No doubt she had relived the event many times and I felt a great swell of sympathy for her.

'What did she say?' urged Holmes, and I too leaned forwards to catch her words and place a comforting hand on hers.

'She said: "Oh, my God, Helen! It was the band. The speckled band!" Then she pointed frantically in the direction of the doctor's room just as he emerged, putting on his dressing gown. When he saw Julia he tried to give her some brandy, but she never regained consciousness. That was the end of my beloved sister.'

'Are you sure about the whistle and the metallic sound?' asked Holmes.

'I swore at the inquiry that I heard them, but the weather was such that … I could have been mistaken.'

'Was your sister dressed?'

'No, sir, she was in her nightdress. She held the stump

of a match in one hand and a
matchbox in the other.'

I knew what that signified. She
had struck a light to see what was
happening in the room when she
raised the alarm.

'What did the coroner say was
the cause of death?' asked Holmes.

'He investigated very thoroughly
but could find no cause. I also
conducted my own investigations.
I found that the door was locked
from the inside, as were the

windows. They had shutters on the outside, reinforced with iron bars. The walls and floor were examined too and they were found to be solid. There is a chimney, but it is always barred. She was alone and looked uninjured.'

'How do you think she died?'

'I believe that she must have died of fear, although I cannot imagine what could have scared her to death like that.'

'What did you think she meant by a "speckled band"?'

Miss Stoner looked thoughtful. 'Sometimes I think it was just her terrified mind playing tricks, and at others I wonder whether she was referring to a band of vagabonds in the grounds. They sometimes wear spotted kerchiefs around their heads.'

'And what has made you come to me now, two years after her death?'

'I, too, have met a man I wish to marry. The wedding is in a few weeks' time.' She blushed a little when she spoke of him and I thought it such a shame that her engagement should be a time of worry and fear rather than joy.

'Two days ago,' she continued, 'some building work began on the west wing of the house. The outside wall of my room was damaged so that I had to move into my sister's room at my step-father's suggestion. I was very reluctant, but there is really no other room that is habitable. I even have to sleep in the very bed in which my sister died. Last night I was lying awake thinking about her when, to my horror,

 I heard the low whistle
again. I sprang up and
lit the lamp but could
see nothing. I was too
frightened to go to bed again so
I stayed awake until dawn and
then slipped out of the house.
I took a dog-cart from the inn
opposite and drove to the station
from where I caught a train to
London, and here I am.'

'Have you told us everything?'
asked Holmes.

She nodded.

'Miss Stoner, you have not.'

Holmes pushed aside the black lace of her frilled cuff to reveal five dark impressions on her right wrist. 'Your step-father has been cruel to you.'

She flushed and covered the bruises which could only have been left by hard fingers. 'Sometimes I think he does not know his own strength.'

For a long time Holmes stared into the crackling fire and I knew better than to interrupt his thoughts. Miss Stoner was less able to relax and fidgeted with her lace cuffs, glancing up at him from time to time.

At last he turned to look at her. 'On the one hand,' he said, 'there is no time to lose, yet there are so many questions left unanswered. If we came to Stoke Moran this afternoon, could we see the rooms without your step-father knowing?'

Miss Stoner nodded. 'He had planned to come to town today on some important business. I expect him to be away all day. We have a housekeeper now but I can ask some errand of her so she will not disturb us.'

'Excellent,' said Holmes, turning to me. 'You are not against coming on this trip are you, Watson?'

'Certainly not,' I said. In truth I was as intrigued as he was. This would make an exciting tale when I came to write it, as I always did after our adventures. Holmes said I was too romantic and prone to embellishing the facts, but I think he was pleased to see his cases put down on paper.

'I have some things to do in

town,' said Miss Stoner, 'and I shall return home on the twelve o'clock train.'

Holmes gave her a small smile. 'I have some business to attend to myself so we shall be with you early this afternoon. Would you care to join us for breakfast?'

'Thank you for the kind offer, but I must go. I'll await your visit this afternoon.'

She seemed more composed and relaxed now that she had told her story, as if a weight had been lifted from her shoulders. Lowering the veil across her face once again, she made her way to the door.

'What do you think of all this, Watson?' Holmes asked when she had gone.

'It seems to be a very dark and sinister business,' I said. 'If it's true that the walls and floor are sound, and the windows, door and chimney were locked and barred, the young lady must have been alone in the room.'

'But what about the whistles and the strange words her sister said before she died?'

'I cannot think,' I replied.

'The key points in this case, as I see it, are these. There are whistles at night and a band of vagabonds in the grounds whom the doctor calls his friends. He seems to want to prevent the young ladies from marrying, since he would have to pay their third of the income that he at present enjoys. Then there's the speckled band and the metallic clang. The bars on the shutters, perhaps ...'

'But what did the vagabonds do?'

'I cannot imagine. That is why I want to go to Stoke Moran today–'

All at once the door crashed open and a huge man filled the doorframe. He was so tall that his hat brushed the top of it. Our visitor wore a top hat, a long frock-coat and high gaiters. In his hand he held a riding crop.

He had a large face covered in a thousand wrinkles, and a tan that would seem to indicate that he had lived for many years in a hot country. His eyes were deep-set and tinged yellow above a long thin nose that made him look like a fierce bird of prey.

Frock-coat and high gaiters
A traditional style of coat with a fitted waist that flares out to just above the knee. A little old-fashioned. Formal ones have a high collar. They are worn by older, rather conservative gentlemen. High leather gaiters on the ankles or lower legs are a mark of a country landowner and not intended as city wear. They are designed to protect riders' trousers and legs when on horseback.

'Which of you is Holmes?' he demanded.

'That is my name,' said Holmes, 'but you have not told me yours.'

'I am Doctor Grimesby Roylott of Stoke Moran.'

'Indeed! Then pray take a seat.'

'I will not! My step-daughter has been here. I followed her. What has she told you?'

'It is a little cold for the time of year,' said Holmes.

'What has she been saying to you?' the old man screamed.

'You cannot put me off.' He took a step forward, shaking his riding crop. 'I have heard of you before. You are Holmes, the meddler.'

My friend smiled.

'Holmes, the busy-body. Holmes, the puppet of Scotland Yard!'

Holmes chuckled heartily. 'You are most entertaining. Please close the door as you leave. There's a draught.'

I was afraid that our visitor was going to explode and I feared for Holmes' safety, yet he seemed to be enjoying himself.

'I will go when I have had my say. I am a dangerous man to meddle with. Keep out of my affairs!'

Roylott stepped forwards and seized the iron poker from the fireplace. Then he bent it into an arc, flung it back into the hearth, and strode out of the room.

'What an amiable fellow,' said Holmes, laughing. 'Had he stayed I could have shown him that though smaller in size I am scarcely lesser in strength.' He picked up the poker and, with a little effort and a quick pull, straightened it out again.

I smiled at his triumph, but hoped that Miss Stoner would not suffer because she had come here.

'Fancy confusing me with the official police force!' Holmes

grumbled. Then, turning to me, he continued. 'Watson, we shall order breakfast and then I shall go out and hope to get more information to help us with this matter.'

I was busy during the rest of the morning in my room writing reports on my patients and it was nearly one o'clock when I heard Holmes return. I put away my work and went down to the sitting room. In his hand he held a sheet of

blue paper that was covered with notes written in his hurried scrawl.

'I have seen the will left by Miss Stoner's mother,' he said. 'The income has decreased in value and is now only £750 a year. If either of the daughters married, they would inherit a third share, that is, £250 a year, leaving the same for Doctor Roylott. Far less than he enjoys at present. He has a very strong motive for not wanting them to marry, does he not, Watson?'

I nodded, turning this new information over in my mind.

Julia's death had not only meant that she would never marry, but also that Roylott had one less person to maintain from his income.

'Are you ready, Watson? Since Doctor Roylott now knows we have an interest in his affairs, we must make haste. We shall call a cab and drive to Waterloo station. I would be obliged if you would put your revolver in your pocket.

Even a man who can twist steel pokers into knots will not argue with that.'

We caught a train for Leatherhead and then hired a carriage for the five-mile journey. It was a beautiful day with a hint of spring to come. The sun was bright and warm and a few fleecy clouds drifted overhead. The trees and hedges were just beginning to show green shoots. There seemed to me to be such a contrast between the sweet promise of spring and the sinister business we were investigating.

Holmes sat in the front of the trap with his arms folded and the peak of his deerstalker hat pulled over his eyes. He seemed to be deep in thought until suddenly he gave a slight jump and then tapped me on the shoulder.

'Look there!' he said.

A wooded park stretched up a slope to a clump of trees and through the trees I could see the

grey gables and high roofs of a
large mansion.

'Stoke Moran?' asked Holmes.

'Yes, sir,' replied the driver.
'That be the house of
Doctor Roylott,
and there's
the village.'

He pointed to a cluster of houses on the left. 'But if you want to get to the house you'll find it shorter to go over this stile and take the footpath. There, where the lady is walking.'

'And that lady is Miss Stoner,' said Holmes, shading his eyes. 'Drop us here, please, driver.'

We got off, paid the fare, and the carriage turned to begin its journey back to Leatherhead. Holmes led the way towards the footpath and held out his hand as the young woman approached.

'Good afternoon, Miss Stoner.'

I thought that she looked much less tense than this morning and even smiled as she shook our hands. 'I have been waiting eagerly for you. As I thought, Doctor Roylott has gone to town. I doubt he will be back until this evening.'

'We have had the pleasure of meeting him already,' said Holmes, and explained in a few words what had happened.

Miss Stoner turned pale. 'Good heavens! He followed me then.'

'Yes,' said Holmes.

'He is so cunning. I never know when I'm safe from him. What will he say when he returns?'

'He will need to guard himself, for there is someone more cunning on his tail. You must lock yourself in tonight. If he is violent then we shall take you to your aunt's in Harrow. Now, I suspect that our time is short, so please take us to the rooms you described. We must begin our investigations.'

We followed her across the field towards the house, which

was built of blotchy grey stone. There was a high central part with a wing curving out on either side like the claws of a crab. The left-hand block was in ruins. The windows were broken and boarded up and the roof caved in. The central part was in better condition and the right-hand wing more modern and obviously the occupied part. There was some scaffolding on the end wall where the stonework had been breached, although no workmen were in sight.

Holmes walked up and down the untidy lawn looking at the windows intently.

'I take it that this was your room.' He pointed to the end room with the scaffolding. 'The centre one was your sister's and the one nearest the central section is Doctor Roylott's chamber.'

'Exactly so,' replied Miss Stoner. 'But now I sleep in the central one.'

'I can't see why there is

need for repairs,' said Holmes. I had been thinking the same thing.

'There is none. I think it was just an excuse to move me from my room.'

Holmes thought for a moment. 'So the other side of this wing, there is a corridor into which these three rooms open.' He referred to the plan she had given us earlier.

Miss Stoner nodded.

'Are there windows in it?'

'Yes, but only very small ones. Too small for anyone to get through.'

'Would you please go into your room and close the shutters?'

I understood that he wanted to see whether it would be possible for anyone to break them open. With no outside access and locked doors on the inside, it seemed impossible that anyone could have got in from the corridor.

Miss Stoner did as requested and Holmes promptly tried and failed to open the shutters. There wasn't even a slit in which to insert a knife and raise the bar.

Then he took out
his magnifying glass
and inspected the
hinges closely. I could
see even with the naked eye
that they were of solid iron and
built into the massive stonework.

Holmes scratched his chin.
'My theory presents some
difficulties. No one could get
through if the shutters were
bolted. Let us see whether the
inside offers more clues.'

Miss Stoner's usual room was
of no interest to Holmes so we

passed it and entered the middle one, in which Miss Stoner was currently sleeping and in which her sister had died. I looked around, trying to see it though Holmes' eyes. It was a plain room with a low ceiling and big open fireplace, though no signs of a recent fire. A brown chest of drawers stood on one side and a narrow bed with a white bedspread on another. There was a dressing table and two wicker chairs beside the window and a carpet in the centre of the room.

The wall panels were of brown, worm-eaten oak and could have been there since the house was built.

Rather a soulless room, I thought. The tragedy of Julia's death hung heavy in our minds.

Holmes sat in one of the chairs and let his eyes roam slowly around the room, taking in every detail of the gloomy surroundings. I did the same, but noticed nothing more than already described.

'Where does the bell ring

through to?' he asked, and I looked and noticed the thick bell-rope for the first time. A not uncommon feature of big houses, it hung beside the bed with the tassel resting on the pillow.

'To the housekeeper's room.'

'It looks newer than everything else.'

Miss Stoner nodded. 'Yes, it was only put in a couple of years ago.'

'At your sister's request?'

'No. There was no one to ring at that time. We always did everything ourselves.'

'It seems a strange thing to install.'

To my surprise, and no doubt Miss Stoner's, Holmes threw himself onto the floor and began to crawl back and forth, examining every inch with his magnifying glass. Then he did the same with

the wooden panelling on
the walls. Stopping by the
bed, he gave the bell-pull a
swift tug.

'It's a dummy!' he said.
'It's not attached to any
wire but just fastened
to a hook near that little
ventilator.'

'I hadn't noticed
that,' I said.

'There are one
or two very strange
things about this
room,' he said.

'What fool of a builder would open a ventilator between rooms? Surely it should open to the outside to allow fresh air into the room.'

'That's also quite recent,' said Miss Stoner.

'Done about the same time as the bell-rope?'

'Yes. There were several little changes done about that time.'

'Hmm,' said Holmes. 'Dummy bell-pulls and ventilators that do not ventilate. With your permission, Miss Stoner, we shall now examine Doctor Roylott's room.'

I followed them to the room next door.

Doctor Roylott's chamber was larger than that of his step-daughter. It, too, was plainly furnished with a small bed, a small shelf of books and one or two chairs. This room, I noticed, also contained a large iron safe. My mind immediately began to consider what it could be used for.

Holmes walked round

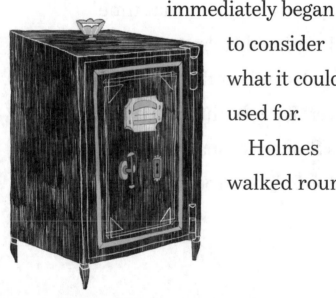

looking at everything, and stopped
at the safe. 'What is in here?' he
asked. Clearly we were thinking
along the same lines.

'My step-father's business
papers.'

'You've seen inside, then?'

'Only once,' said Miss Stoner,
'several years ago. It was full of
documents.'

'There isn't a cat in it?'

'No. What a strange idea.'

Holmes pointed to a small bowl
of milk on top of the safe. 'Look at
this!'

'No, we don't keep a cat. Just a cheetah and a baboon.'

'Well, a cheetah is a big cat but a saucer of milk would not go very far in satisfying its thirst.' Holmes squatted in front of a wooden chair and examined the seat with interest. He smiled in satisfaction. 'I believe that I have found everything I was looking for. Thank you.' He stood and returned the magnifying glass to his pocket. Holmes turned as if ready to leave before suddenly pausing.

'Hello! Here is something interesting!'

What had caught his eye was a dog leash hanging on a corner of the bed. It was tied to make a loop.

'What do you make of that, Watson?'

'It's just a common leash,' I said. 'But I don't know why it should be tied like that.'

'Ah me!' said Holmes with a sigh. 'It's a wicked world, and when a clever man turns his brains to crime it is the worst of all.

I think I have seen enough, Miss Stoner.' With that, he turned on his heel and left the room.

I had never seen my friend's face so grim or his brow so dark.

We went outside onto the lawn and eagerly awaited what Holmes would say next. Miss Stoner and I watched as he walked around the lawn several times, deep in thought. Neither of us were willing to interrupt him so we had no choice but to wait.

After several minutes he

turned to our client. 'It is absolutely essential, Miss Stoner, that you should follow my advice in every respect.'

'I shall certainly do so,' she said. 'I am in your hands.'

'Firstly, my friend and I must spend the night in your room.'

Both Miss Stoner and I gazed at him in astonishment.

'Let me explain,' said Holmes. 'I believe that is the village inn over there.' He pointed across the park.

'Yes, it's the Crown.'

'And your windows would be visible from there?'

'Certainly.'

'Then you must lock yourself in your room saying you have a headache. When you hear Doctor Roylott go to his room, open the shutters of your window and put your lamp there

 as a signal to us. Then go into your old room. Can you sleep there for one night?'

She nodded. 'But what will you do?'

'We shall spend the night in your room and investigate the noise that has disturbed you.'

Noticing the confidence with which Holmes gave his instructions, Miss Stoner replied, 'I believe, Mr Holmes, that you already have the answer to this mystery.'

'Perhaps,' he said.

'Then please tell me what caused my sister's death.'

'I prefer to have absolute proof before I speak.'

'Do you think she died of fright?' She looked up at him earnestly.

'No, I do not think so. I am sure it was a more definite cause. But we must go now before Doctor Roylott gets back. If he finds us here, then the whole thing would be lost. Remember that you must do as I have instructed. If you do so, you may be sure that we will overcome the danger threatening you.'

'Goodbye, and be brave,' I said, laying a hand on Miss Stoner's arm. She gave me a small smile and we departed to the inn.

We booked into an upstairs

room with windows facing the manor. At dusk we saw Doctor Roylott drive past, his huge figure towering over the boy who drove him. When the boy had difficulty opening the rusty gates, we heard the roar

of Roylott's voice and saw him shake his fist at the poor boy.

The carriage disappeared from our view and a few minutes later we saw the glow of a lamp appear in one of the sitting rooms.

'Do you know, Watson,' said Holmes, turning to me, 'I am worried about you coming with me tonight because there is certainly an element of danger.'

'But can I be of assistance?'

'Most certainly,' he said.

'Then I shall come. But, Holmes, you speak of danger so

you must have seen more in those rooms than I did.'

'I probably deduced more. I saw no more than you did.'

'I saw nothing unusual except for the bell-pull, and I cannot imagine what it is used for.'

'You saw the ventilator too?'

'Yes, but strange as it may be, not so much as a small rat could pass through.'

'I knew that we should find a ventilator before

we even arrived at Stoke Moran,'
said Holmes mysteriously.

'My dear Holmes, how could
you?'

'You remember Miss Stoner
saying that her sister could smell
Doctor Roylott's
cigar? That
suggested at once that there must
be some opening between the
two rooms. It had to be a small
one otherwise it would have been
mentioned at the coroner's enquiry.'

I shook my head. 'What harm
can there be in that?'

'A curious coincidence of dates, Watson. A ventilator is made, a cord is hung, and a lady sleeping in the bed dies.'

'I cannot see any connection.'

'Did you notice anything strange about the bed?'

'No.'

'It was clamped to the floor. Have you ever heard of anyone bolting their bed to the floor?'

I had not.

'The lady could not move her bed. It must always be in the same relative position to the ventilator and the dummy bell-pull.'

'Holmes,' I said. 'I seem to see dimly what you are hinting at. We are just in time to prevent a clever and horrible crime.'

'Clever enough and horrible enough,' agreed Holmes. 'When a doctor does wrong he is the foremost of criminals. He has nerve and he has knowledge. We shall have horrors enough before the night is through. Let us rest for a few hours and turn our minds to something cheerful.'

Holmes and I ate a passable meal in the dining room and then sat in our room in quiet contemplation or looking at the newspaper. We kept our

The Times

3rd April 1883

DRAYCOTT AVENUE MURDER

The case of the missing slipper has been resolved due to the excellent work of our police force.

Assisted by Mr Sherlock Holmes, an amateur detective, the item was found concealed in the same room as the deceased. The butler of the household was arrested earlier today. It is reported that the servant was conducting an affair with Mr Smythe's daughter and killed his employer after an angry confrontation.

drapes open and at about nine o'clock the light beyond the trees was put out and all was dark at the manor.

Two more hours passed slowly and at about eleven o'clock a single bright light glowed.

'That is our signal,' said Holmes, rising from his chair. 'It is coming from the middle window.'

He and I went downstairs, and told the landlord that we were going to visit an acquaintance and may be out all night. Then we ventured out into the night, a chill wind blowing in our faces as we headed towards the one yellow light twinkling to guide us on our solemn errand.

It was not difficult to enter the grounds because the wall was broken down in places. We made our way through the trees, crossed the lawn, and were about to enter through the window when some hideous creature darted from a laurel bush, rolled on the grass with its limbs

writing, and then disappeared
into the darkness.

'My God, did you see that?' My
heart was thumping and Holmes
had grasped my wrist in a vice-

like grip,
but he soon
relaxed it
and gave a
low laugh.

'That is the baboon,' he said.

I had quite forgotten about the strange pets that roamed the grounds and my heart thumped even faster when I remembered the other creature on the loose – a cheetah, surely many times worse than a baboon. At any moment it could spring on us from the darkness of the trees. I could not get into the bedroom fast enough.

We both removed our shoes and Holmes quietly closed the shutters and moved the lamp back onto the table. Everything appeared the same as it had earlier in the day. Then he whispered in my ear so quietly that I could hardly hear. 'The least sound would be fatal to our plans.'

I nodded.

'We must sit without a light,' he whispered again. 'He would see it through the ventilator.'

I nodded again, wondering what we were waiting for but certain I would know when it came. It was a truly nerve-racking experience that I had so eagerly agreed to undertake.

'Do not go to sleep,' went on Holmes, his cupped mouth to my ear. 'Your life may depend upon it. And have your gun ready in case we need it. I will sit at the head of the bed and you in the chair.'

I had almost forgotten about the gun but took it out and laid it on the table. Holmes had brought a long, thin cane, which he placed on the bed beside him.

Next to it he put a box of matches and the stump of a candle. Then he turned down the lamp and we sat in darkness.

How could I ever forget that awful night? I could not hear a sound, not even Holmes breathing, and yet I knew that he sat alert a few feet in front of me, probably in the same state of nervous tension as me. I wished that whatever event was to come would happen soon.

With the shutters closed
there was absolute darkness.
From outside there came the
occasional call of a bird and
once, right outside the window,
a long drawn-out whine of a cat,
revealing that the cheetah was on
the prowl.

Far away, every quarter of an
hour, the parish clock chimed.
Twelve midnight struck, then one,
then two, then three o'clock. How
long those hours were. And still
we sat waiting for whatever was
going to happen.

All at once there was a gleam
of light from the ventilator.
It flickered like candlelight.

I gasped and
heard Holmes
stiffen. My hand
moved towards my
gun although I had no
idea what I might be shooting at.
There was a strong smell of
burning oil and the light steadied
and dimmed a little. Someone in
the next room had lit a lantern
with a shutter across it to dim
the light. I heard a tiny sound

of movement that then stopped.
I was aware that I was holding
my breath and released it slowly,
trying my best not to make
a sound. I wanted to change
position on the chair but was
afraid to move in case I made my
presence known.

For half an hour I stayed
motionless, straining my ears, my
nerves alert. Then I heard a sound.
A very gentle, soothing sound, like
the hiss of a boiling kettle.

At that sound, Holmes sprang
from the bed, struck a match, and

lashed furiously at the
bell-pull with his cane.

'Did you see it,
Watson?' he shouted.
'Did you see it?'

But I had seen
nothing. What had
happened? What
had I missed?

At the same
moment that
Holmes struck
the match

I heard a whistle, long and low, just as Miss Stoner had described, but the light had temporarily blinded me. All I could see was my friend's face, deathly pale and filled with horror and loathing.

He had stopped thrashing at whatever it was and was gazing up at the ventilator when there was a sound that made my heart almost leap from my chest. It was a horrible cry – a cry of fear and pain and anger that got louder and louder until I was almost forced to put my hands over my ears.

The cry was so loud and long that I was sure people in the village would have been roused from their sleep. It struck such cold in my heart that I know it will stay with me forever.

I stood looking at Holmes and he at me until the last echoes of that terrible shriek had died away.

'What can it mean?' I asked when at last I could speak.

'It means that it is all over,' Holmes answered. 'And perhaps, after all, it is for the best. Bring your gun, Watson, and we will enter Doctor Roylott's room.'

He lit the lamp and I followed him out into the corridor. Twice he hammered on Doctor Roylott's door but there was no reply from within. Then he turned the handle and went in with me close behind, my gun at the ready, not knowing what I was going to see.

On the table stood the lantern with one of the shutters half open so that the beam shone on the iron safe, the door of which hung partly open.

Beside the table, seated on

a wooden chair, was Doctor Roylott. He was dressed in a grey dressing gown and he had red slippers on his feet. Across his lap lay the dog leash that we had seen earlier in the day. His face was tilted upward towards the ventilator, fixing it with the most dreadful stare. Round his forehead was a strange brownish-yellow speckled band, tightly wound. He made no movement or sound as we entered.

'The band! The speckled band!' whispered Holmes.

I took a step forward. In an instant the strange head-piece began to move and then reared itself from amongst his hair. The flat diamond-shaped head rose up and its neck puffed out like a huge hood. It was a snake!

'It's a swamp adder!'
said Holmes.

'The deadliest snake in India.
He has died within ten seconds
of being bitten. His own weapon
has turned upon him.'

I looked at the creature in
horror and shuddered. It was
all beginning to make sense now.
What an evil and loathsome man
Doctor Roylott had been!

Holmes carefully took the leash

from Roylott's lap. 'Let us get this creature back into its den and then we can take Miss Stoner to a place of safety and inform the police.'

He deftly threw the noose around the reptile's neck, pulled it tight and, carrying it at arm's length, threw it into the iron safe and slammed the door shut.

Miss Stoner had been awoken by the noise and stood, shaking, in the corridor outside her room.

'You are safe now, Miss Stoner,' said Holmes, taking her hand in a rare moment of compassion. 'But I'm afraid that your step-father is dead.'

Her eyes widened in surprise rather than grief but she said nothing.

'We must inform the police,' said Holmes. 'If Watson will stay with you and make a cup of tea, I shall rouse someone at the inn and ask them to take a message.'

I nodded and we led her into the kitchen where the wood range still gave off some warmth. When she was seated and I had stoked up the fire to boil a kettle, Holmes left. 'What happened?'

the young lady asked after a long period of silence.

I shook my head. 'I'll let Holmes explain the details to you. All I can say is that you were right that your step-father meant you harm, but he is dead and you have nothing else to fear. Your nightmare is over.'

She seemed to relax and sipped her tea until Holmes  returned. I offered him a cup but he refused, seating himself opposite Miss Stoner.

'It seems that the baboon and the cheetah were not the only wild animals that Doctor Roylott kept here,' he began. 'He had also brought a snake from India: a swamp adder.'

Miss Stoner stared at him in horror. 'The most deadly snake …' she said.

Holmes continued. 'I admit that after our meeting at Baker Street I had developed a theory that turned out to be incorrect. The presence of the gangs in the grounds and your sister's use of the word 'band' to describe what she saw that night were enough to send me down the wrong path. Once we had seen the rooms, however, it became clear that nothing could enter through the window or the door.

When I first saw the ventilator and the dummy bell-pull I knew that they were significant. I also noticed that the bed was clamped to the floor so that it could not be moved from beneath the

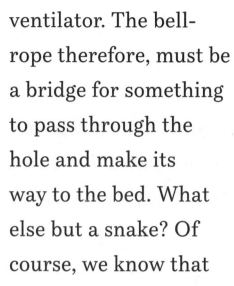

ventilator. The bell-
rope therefore, must be
a bridge for something
to pass through the
hole and make its
way to the bed. What
else but a snake? Of
course, we know that
he brought several
animals back
from India. The
snake was part
of that collection,
although he kept it
hidden. Its poison

is quick-acting yet impossible to trace by the police laboratories. Being a doctor in India, Roylott would have known that. I imagine that he must have treated patients who had been bitten by such a creature. The coroner carrying out the investigation would have had to be sharp-eyed to see the puncture marks of the bite. It is doubtful that he would have even considered such a possibility.'

Miss Stoner had a strange expression on her face, something between sadness and disbelief, as if, even though she had not liked her step-father, she couldn't believe that he could do such a thing to get his hands on her and her sister's money.

'He could not allow the snake to remain in the room, as it would have been discovered the following morning. He must have trained it to return at the sound of the whistle, with the lure of the milk,' Holmes continued. 'And an inspection of the chair showed that he often stood on it, which he would have to do to reach the ventilator.'

'I was lucky that first night,' said Miss Stoner. 'He must have sent it through. I wonder that it didn't bite me.'

'He was in no great hurry,' said Holmes. 'the snake may not bite the bed's occupant every time, but he knew that sooner or later it would happen. As long as it happened before your wedding.'

'And you remember the metallic clang you heard?' I put in. 'He kept the snake in the safe.'

She looked from one to the other of us. 'I cannot thank you

enough, Mr Holmes and Doctor Watson. You risked your lives tonight. I assume you waited for the snake to come through the ventilator?'

'Indeed,' said Holmes, 'and then I beat it with my stick until it was driven back through its hole. We had the advantage of knowing what to expect. Some of my strikes hit the creature and angered it, which is why it flew at the first person it saw - its master.'

We did not have to wait long for morning and, as soon as Miss Stoner had packed a bag, we took her to the station and saw her onto a train bound for her aunt's in Harrow.

After putting the whole affair into the hands of the police, we then made our way back to Baker Street. The mystery was over. This time the coroner gave the cause of death as: Doctor Roylott, of Stoke Moran, died while playing with a dangerous pet. The true details of the

case were to be known only to the
three of us - Holmes and I,
and Miss Stoner. I sincerely hope

that the details would fade from her mind once she was married and enveloped in the loving care of her new husband.

Sherlock Holmes

World-renowned private detective Sherlock Holmes has solved hundreds of mysteries, and is the author of such fascinating monographs as *Early English Charters* and *The Influence of a Trade Upon the Form of a Hand*. He keeps bees in his free time.

Dr John Watson

Wounded in action at Marwan, Dr John Watson left the army and moved into 221B Baker Street. There he was surprised to learn that his new friend, Sherlock Holmes, faced daily peril solving crimes, and began documenting his investigations. Dr Watson also runs a doctor's practice.